D1450027

MIGHTY MIKE
BUILDS A Nature Trail

By Kelly Lynch   Illustrated by Casey Lynch

magic
Wagon

visit us at www.abdopublishing.com

For Ian, who loves big machines —KL
For Jack —CL

Published by Magic Wagon, a division of the ABDO Group, 8000 West 78th Street, Edina, Minnesota 55439.

Printed in the United States of America, North Mankato, Minnesota.
092010
012011
 This book contains at least 10% recycled materials.

Written by Kelly Lynch
Illustrations by Casey Lynch
Edited by Stephanie Hedlund and Rochelle Baltzer
Cover and interior layout and design by Abbey Fitzgerald

Library of Congress Cataloging-in-Publication Data

Lynch, Kelly, 1976-
    Mighty Mike builds a nature trail / by Kelly Lynch ; illustrated by Casey Lynch.
        p. cm. -- (Mighty Mike)
    ISBN 978-1-61641-130-5
  [1. Building--Fiction. 2. Helpfulness--Fiction. 3. Community life--Fiction.] I. Lynch, Casey, ill. II. Title.
    PZ7.L9848Mbn 2011
    [E]--dc22

                                    2010016268

Early Monday morning, Mighty Mike was startled by a loud banging on his office door. *Who could that be?* Mike wondered as he glanced at the clock. "Come in," he finally hollered when the banging didn't stop.

The door swung open and a dashing figure in a green uniform stood before Mike.

"My name is Ranger Woods," the stranger told Mike. "I'm from the Forest and Parks Service. We want you to build a nature trail to the top of Mount Impossible."

"Mount Impossible?" Mighty Mike asked nervously. "But I've never built a nature trail."

"Luckily, I have the plans," Ranger Woods barked as he handed Mike the blueprints. "Good luck," he added, then sharply turned and walked out.

Mighty Mike unrolled the blueprints. Yikes! Mike thought as he leafed through them. *How will I ever get to the top of Mount Impossible? There are creeks to cross and canyons to climb!*

Mighty Mike put his head in his hands and sighed. Mike thought of his dear old grandpa. If he learned anything from his dear old grandpa it was that you'll never know what you can do unless you try.

The next day, Mighty Mike started up the mountain with his excavator. He had never built a nature trail, but he knew he had to try. At first the work was easy, but before long Mike came to his first problem.

A roaring river raged down Mount Impossible, and the nature trail would have to cross it. Mighty Mike scratched his head, wondering what to do.

"I've got it!" he finally yelled. There was a long, flat boulder lying next to the trail. Mighty Mike picked it up with his excavator and laid it across the river, creating a perfect bridge.

A little farther up the mountain, Mighty Mike came to an even bigger problem. The nature trail would have to cross a narrow canyon. Mike again scratched his head, wondering what to do.

I'll have to build another bridge, he decided.

Mike cut six tall trees, then carefully set them across the canyon with his excavator. When they were in place, he bolted them together and nailed solid planks across the bottom. Then, he added railings.

Mighty Mike continued up Mount Impossible. The creek and the canyon were behind him and the top was in sight. Mike thought the rest would be easy. But then he came to the biggest problem yet.

Right before the top of Mount Impossible was a rock wall. It was 100 feet tall, and there was no way around it. Mighty Mike sat down to think. The more he thought, the more he realized that he couldn't go any farther.

I guess I'll have to give up, Mike thought with a frown. *I just can't make it to the top.*

But as Mighty Mike headed down Mount Impossible, he couldn't get his dear old grandpa's words out of his head. Mike knew he had to give it one more try. He turned around and looked at the rock wall with determination. The more he looked, the more determined he felt.

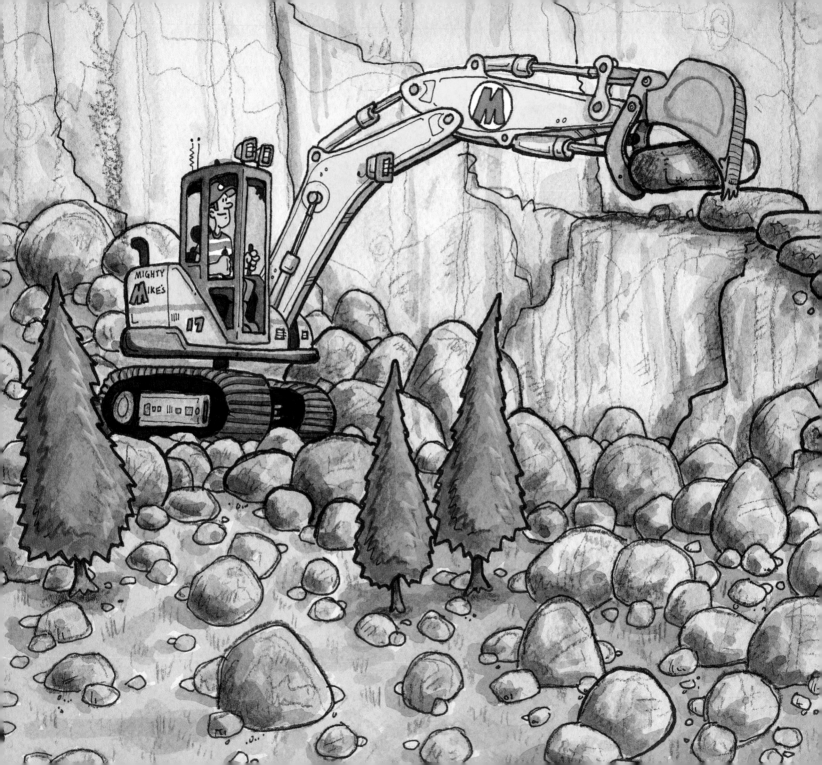

Mike decided he would build a staircase with huge boulders to get to the top. Up, up, up Mike went, using the boulders that covered Mount Impossible for stairs.

When Mighty Mike finally made it to the top, he was amazed by what he saw. The view was breathtaking! To the north were the tallest mountains he'd ever seen. To the west were the endless waves of the Pacific Ocean. To the east were glimmering green forests. And to the south a golden prairie seemed to stretch forever.

If I hadn't tried I would have never seen this, thought Mighty Mike. His dear old grandpa would have been proud. Mike imagined all the happy families that would walk up the nature trail he built. He smiled as he climbed into his excavator and started down the mountain. With any luck, he'd make it home before dark.

Glossary

blueprints - detailed plans for building something.

boulder - a large, rounded rock that isn't connected to the ground.

canyon - a deep valley with steep sides and a stream running through it.

determination - the act of deciding on an action firmly.

excavator - a power-operated shovel.

What Would Mighty Mike Do?

• Why does Mighty Mike think he can't build the nature trail?

• What makes Mighty Mike change his mind?

• What problems does Mighty Mike run into on the trail?

• How does Mighty Mike feel when the nature trail is finished?